everything i couldn't say

A catalogue record for this book is available from the National Library of Australia

To those who found
a star on a cloudy night

everything i couldn't say

Isabella Juanita Lyn

Playlists

Book

Grade 7

Grade 8

Grade 9

Grade 10

Grade 11

Grade 12

Grade 7

I wouldn't have chosen to be close to you

It was too early in the year for me
to be in a race,
my horrific relationship,
in all my years of schooling
since the sweet age of five.

It wasn't any different
to the other races I've run;
why did I think a new school
meant new experiences?

Let down by a single thought...

You were not a beacon,
saving me from the tunnel of loneliness,
or a potential friend from the blue
I could've leaned on in this new marathon.

You were a moment...
of despair,
turned into lifelong misery.

The instant I sat in that chair
in my History lesson,
I knew
I'd never sit there again.

But my plan faltered before it began.

I was stuck next to you,
needing to talk, whisper
and learn with you by my side,
while my internal thoughts ran laps.

Was this an endless loop
trapping me,
preventing me
from escaping you?

I *didn't* like being close to you.
                                        I *liked* being close to you.
I *cried* from being close to you.
                                        I *wept* being away from you.
I *hated* being close to you.
                                        I *yearned* for every moment with you.

If I had another choice that fateful day,
I wouldn't have chosen to be close to you.

My heart was racing

The constant beating was the starting pistol,
the start of anxiety's eternal effect,
because of you and your first rumour.

Lub dub lub dub lub dub lub dub dub-dub.

It felt like a battle...
I could never win
and didn't want to lose.
I moved away from you
and felt safe for a few weeks,
from my ruins.

Lub dub lub dub lub dub lub dub dub-dub.

But another unfortunate
fateful day
brought you to me,

my heart racing
when you ran alongside me.

Lub dub lub dub lub dub lub dub dub-dub.

How did you know I was at a debate?
Surprise,
an electric shock,

fireworks and sunlight,
the starting pistol caught me off-guard.

Rivals didn't have connections.

     Lub dub lub dub lub dub lub dub dub-dub.

I avoided you
to please,
     to ease,
          to calm
my competitive heart —
only to have caught you in my first place.

An easy win with your athletic background
but a blessing of victorious triumph
in disguise; you took my blue ribbon
made from an invisible thread
connecting you
to my heart.

     Lub dub lub dub lub dub lub dub dub-dub.

You shook my hand
after I grabbed your red ribbon.
          I gasped!
I didn't like having your ribbon in my hand
nor how your smile made me feel
and would make me feel for many more races.

I wish it was in your hand.
Was that smile for me?

Lub dub lub dub lub dub lub dub dub-dub.

You became a friend afterwards,
One at last! I wanted more.
one I relied on and trusted.
Oh, more!
But you knew it was a façade
How tragic!
to keep my heart racing.
Even more tragic!

Lub dub lub dub lub dub lub dub dub-dub.

Like your first handwritten letter in my hand.

Lub dub lub dub lub dub lub dub dub-dub...

I wanted some space

I thought running was over
but you hid a letter in my shade,
forcing me into flaming rays
like an intruding hare
running farther and
farther away from the finish line.

I'd have run away
from you if I could
but you'd catch me
as I was drowning
from your eyes,
smiles and lips,
my heated blood
against your chest,
stopping the blur of
heavenly... *you.*

I wanted some   space   from you
but you became a sustained force,
like a transcendental divide.

You became a supply
of trust I craved,
one I demanded daily
without thought.

We were in an imperfect equilibrium.

That day, I wanted to speak out
and you decided to silence me.

Your shield drowned my worries
but inflicted the greatest burn one could imagine.
Trust was stones and water,
unstable like the graphs of sine and cosine.

I had no clue — what was true or false
almost like a repelling force.

You weren't
a welcoming sight
once I awoke,
but a gruesome,
grotesque figure
I kneeled
below.

Inconsistent declarations were once fine,
a little trauma-filled phoenix screeching
from its confines,
watching the ashes
smoulder your love and affection.

I *wanted* to run from you.
But I was starting to see stars,

hope,
longing.

My legs were getting tired
but I
couldn't,
wouldn't,
shouldn't
fall into your arms,
a haven from pre-race nightmares
and a relief from the questions in my head.

You were the one who waited,
stayed and remained.
You didn't rush off into the abyss
but you were amiss to us.

I knew I shouldn't
be close to you
after you broke my trust
like it was a sliver of dust...

But I didn't have anyone else
to lean on
but you...

I knew it was a weakness,

but you cared,

even if
momentarily.
I thought I wanted space
but I wanted to be close to you,

only you,
forever you.

The race ceased behind us.

Who were we?

Those moments meant nothing to you
when you lied to my face.
You knew so much about me;
I knew so little about you...

What friendship
did we hold?

What friendship
did we build?

What friendship
did we create?

What friendship
did I have with you?

You were a fire
lighting my imagination,
allowing me
to embrace who I was
in a ghostly place.
You made me feel
like I belonged
for once
only to
painfully extract that

for *your* calculated race

and inflict a burn
like the Ancient Ashes of Regret.

I trusted you —
that wasn't enough.

I cared for you,
protected you
when you got hurt —
I was always there!

You hurt me,
tears ran.

You shut me away like second-place ribbons,
a phoenix captive from flight.
But your letters stayed on my desk
waiting,
waiting,
waiting for the flame.

Grade 8

You were at my door

I couldn't believe my eyes.
Why were you at my door?
Why did you haunt my home?
Where was "goodbye" two months ago?

A phantom of love roamed my walls.

I needed closure.
I didn't want closure from you,
especially unannounced
over the summer
when I was trying to heal from you
and those memories
that turned my life into a nightmare,
adding to my frail health and mind.

I couldn't speak,
I couldn't think,
I couldn't be myself
when I saw you,
dressed casually
unlike your monster in disguise.

Girls passed by and gushed over you
while I resisted the urge to roll my eyes,
vomit onto your shoes and shut the door.

I should've kept my eyes closed and slammed the door.

"You needed to let go" — you said

Well, I would've if I could.
Stop acting like you controlled me
when you knew I was a force
you collided with.

It hurt when you thought
I wasn't okay
when I was almost over you
and now you were on my doorstep.

So much for forgetting the one thing I didn't need...

"You needed to let go," you always said.
Why bother explaining when actions spoke
louder than your flightless words?

I guess I'd have appreciated an eviction notice,
but you didn't have the brain for that.

Did you have to come to my door tonight?
I burned your letters,
deleted your number, calls
and texts.

I destroyed you but you DEMOLISHED me.

Good or bad, I didn't know

I dreaded the first day back
(not knowing if we shared classes).
Thankfully, we shared one class
and I almost saw you run.

My friends still didn't know what you did to me
and I preferred it,
(but they'd learn the truth soon).
I still wanted to defend you
despite it disabling me in the end.

What friendship couldn't last one argument?

I remembered letting go and hanging out again.

And my friends caught my eye —
the most intense conversation.

But care was long gone.
I lived through confused faces,
distaste and concerns.
I didn't owe anyone an explanation of our friendship.

I lost my friends that day but it was crucial to future-me.

Your friends soon became mine.

It was a nice group to be a part of,
safe,
from the race of mystery
and insecurity.

I cried many times during those first few months
but you were there when my tears blinked away,
holding me tightly and telling me everything would be
okay.

I didn't want to lose our friendship,
now my necklace from our city outing.

Was this friendship
good or bad,
I didn't know.

When I was alone, my mind felt safe

You could've lied to me about the horrid jokes
when your friends called over the holidays,
and I could've lied to you about my pain
when I wanted to be alone with my thoughts.
I guess we were liars for different reasons.
You didn't want to hurt their feelings
and I needed to recharge my social battery.

I couldn't recall the last race I ran alone
and this one was neck and neck.
I needed a breather, but if I took one,
you'd sprint off with the wind,
leaving me to inhale your asthmatic dust.

Sadness, anger, denial

I didn't want to cry anymore,
I didn't want to feel anymore,
I didn't want to care anymore.

You didn't want to let me go,
you didn't want to scream "Let it go,"
you didn't want to see me go.

Was our friendship sadness
and anger
and denial?

A waterfall

You happened again.
All over again.

I thought the tricks were over,
but I was living in a fairy-tale
while you wrote those lies into reality.

A ruthless, tyrannical reality.

You liked breaking my trust
and trying to earn it again.
Why did I let you get to me?
Why did I keep trusting you?
Was I attached to
our more-fragile-than-glass friendship?

A see-through, uncomplicated glass.

I ran towards the waterfall over the cliff,
feeling the pull of the current reach out
and drag me in.

You held my arm,
fighting the current,
bringing me into your embrace
and running towards
a newfound target,

no longer the finish line.

The night fell around us like a blanket,
woven by the fabricated threads of my world,
and you finally placed my feet on the ground.
The cliff wobbled and the chilled mists danced,
the hairs on my arm standing.

I didn't want your offered jacket.

My foot slipped into the soft, warm blanket.
You held me in shadowed safety.

I wanted to continue running
but you asked me to stay.
I could have run and gotten
a bit of distance between us
but my heart couldn't bring my legs to.

You asked me if I was okay.
I lied through chattering teeth.
You held my necklace,
smoothing the engraved heart.
It was the reason you chose it,
my favourite charm.

"Why did you run towards the waterfall?"
"Why wouldn't I run towards the waterfall?"

Your head dropped in annoyance,
no surprise hearing your defeated sigh.

"Did you ever care about me?"

"Nothing was more precious than you,
and I was never going to take that for granted.
But I pushed your buttons and trust."

Our friendship flowed like our trust issues.

My head pounded like fireworks

You were once the crowd at the start of a race,
now a constant ringing in my ears.

I once loved the gorgeous fireworks of the city,
now a sour taste in my mouth.

You were once the fuzzy feeling in my heart,
now a stone hammer, softening my deathbed.

I once loved blasting music,
now I dreamt of a silenced world.

You were the reason

I almost lost myself.
My beliefs,
dreams
and values.

What were you doing to me?

You almost destroyed your reputation.
Your life,
goals
and plans.

Who were you becoming?

We weren't ~~good~~ for each other.

"You didn't deserve this" — my mind

I lived through your endless lies,
forming regrets that scrutinised my being.
I should've let you go and cut all ties,
but here I was knocking on your door
with *another* handwritten note.

"You didn't deserve this," whispered my mind.

But this note meant more than my mind knew.

My mouth was sewn

The year drew to a close before I knew
my heart was beating faster around you.

"You okay?" concerned eyes replicated my heart.

"Yeah, *I'm fine*," a whisper carried by the summer breeze.

Was it the way you kept me on my toes?
Or the way you earned my trust easier than most?
Maybe it was the way our rivalry was more than hate.

I couldn't look you in the eye
from fear, panic, or something else.
But I felt safe with you and the monster inside.

Your arm draped around me while we watched the
New Year's Eve fireworks and serenity became hope.
Your fingers found the heart charm,
running over the engraving
while your voice wished,

"I love you."

Grade 9

A slight escape

Your confession was bittersweet.

We were apart for months
and I couldn't process anything.
Did I see you that way?
I doubted
but I couldn't fault it.

Maybe you were cute
but I didn't love you.
Your calls, texts and voicemails
made me miss you more
but a slight escape
from the soon-awkward confrontation.

I never responded over those months,
but you continued amusing me with messages
keeping me up at night when books failed.

I feared the start of a crush.

But I couldn't like you
even if I wanted to.

But why else did I stop teachers
from giving you detention
because you misbehaved

in class?

Or when you used your phone
after the new school policy
forbid them from the grounds?

And when you accidentally bullied a junior
and I cancelled your suspension?

But when I terminated your expulsion, it was crystal
clear.

I love you
but I never *loved* you.

I wanted to shout

Seeing you again
brought adrenaline.
You embraced me
like nothing happened
but the air was different,
at least for me.

I didn't want to worry you,
hiding behind my smile
while my heart raged on.

You told me about your plans for the year
and how nothing could've stopped you this time.
Your determined gaze shot my heart,

hurting my soul since you couldn't
have felt how I felt for you.

I did like you more than a friend.

All because of our silly rivalry.

No classes this year,
my old dream came true.

But your friends overheard my new insane feelings
and I hated their endless teasing sprinting in my ears.

You were gone and me done.
Never did love have an answer;
"I wanted to shout," said my troubled heart.

Muted.

Insults floated in my head

How did you tell someone you were hurting
when their truth was unbelievable?
How did you tell someone the grazed wound
slashed from tireless ignorance?

Your friends betrayed my trust,
my secret was out.
I couldn't face you
but you never hid your face.

Couldn't you have ended my humiliation?

Insults floated through my mind,
watching you laugh along,
my heart shattered
bit by bit.

You didn't believe them,
relief and regret.
I knew I shouldn't have
let myself fall but

I couldn't stop myself from drowning.
And now I was stuck in a bottomless pit of tears.

What once was so beautiful was a lie.

That was the bitter truth.

Your words cut my confidence

You destroyed my self-esteem
but what was I expecting when you
were he two years ago?

Confidence was gone
but differently this time,
not fear or panic.

Pain and insecurity.

I couldn't stop my heart from wanting,
pleading, hoping and yearning
for you to be more than a friend
while my head wanted you to be nothing.

You let me down more than once
so why was this time different?

"I never loved you," cut me.

I wanted to hide away

The year was over painfully slow
and I was glad I could disappear from you.
Those final months were traumatic,
learning the truth and your honest feelings.
You never cared, never wanted to care.
I was your scapegoat, fooling competitors
for your benefit when everyone failed.
But the worst part of this year was when
you pulled me aside, gave me a note,
and smiled nervously while I read,

"I love you."

Grade 10

You restored those unbreakable walls

These holidays should've been different,
filled with heartbreak, loss and grief.

But they weren't.

These holidays shouldn't have been
momentous, wondrous and magical.

Yet they were.

You restored my unbreakable walls,
but at what cost for the truth?

I didn't want to still love you but how
could I have left when I needed you?

I didn't want to still hold you close
but how could I have moved on when
you still loved me and kept me as yours?

You restored my unbreakable walls
and I was yours in my heart alone.

You annoyed my heartstrings

At first in an irritating way,
yet now my favourite quality.
You were always maddening.

Nothing you did ever
got on my nerves unlike
before when we were
at each other's throats
where hate was the only way
to describe how we felt.

But here we were laughing,
with your hand in mine and mine
holding yours, forever entwined.

You annoyed my heartstrings
but it was your way of saying
"I love you like no other."

But who knew of the poison?

Another bowl, another strike

Remember that day
you told me
you loved me
and it seemed so true
in the moment?

Remember that day
you handed me a note about
your 'everlasting love' for me
which surpassed the truth?

It burned brighter than the necklace in the moonlight.

You took another bowl,
another strike the day
you held her hand in front of me,
smiling like she
was your world
and I was a figment
of your past.

Remember that day
you said I was your
'*Only One*'
and it was too good to be true
and my gut knew?

Remember that day
you promised me
I was yours
and you smashed
my glass heart
against the rocks?

The necklace smashed fragments of my bones.

I knew it was over for us
when I saw you with her,
realising we were never anything
except for a fantasy I
conjured in my mind
along with a forgotten dream.

You didn't want me
other than getting you out of mischief.
You didn't want me
other than helping you fool superiors.

You took another bowl, another strike
at the small crack in my heart
you almost healed but

spl   it.

"I dared you to speak of your pain."

You couldn't have accepted you damaged me before,
yet you were fooling me into believing you apologised
for your actions but couldn't dare stop from choosing
her.

My heart needed a break, one from you
and your twisted manipulation because I couldn't run
farther if you saw an injured contender.

You wanted me to speak my pain to you, but I knew you.
I wasn't falling for it again, not after every race hitherto.
You wanted my pain; you should've taken my "goodbye".

Acceptance was a lie

I thought I was over you —
I was in denial.
Little did I know this
only began a long
journey to forget
you.

Grade 11

Alone finally

Summer was lonely.

The first time I had to
fix my heartbreak and
end the lingering hurt.

My mind battled
for a consolation
I didn't want.

I should've trusted past-me.

Present-me was a fool in love.
I couldn't have been worse
than a blind, hopeless romantic.

But I was so much worse.

That summer was one of isolation.

It was my first of many.
I didn't know what to do,
who to talk to, who to trust.
I was so bored with my eternal sadness
and everything was quiet.

I became helpless that summer —

all because of you —

January 17th.

The first time my heartbreak became evident
and the first time I knew you were gone.

January 17th.

I remembered that coughing fit
but I remembered you,
those tears —

the race that ended all races.

Was this worth my energy?

The first week was brutal
and I had seventy more.
Was this worth my energy,
running from you and her

every second?

Drained by the day,
disregarding my work until late,
wishing for my strength
to complete everything left.

It didn't help our timetables collided
and I had to see you at every turn.
It was worse having classes
with *your only true love*.

Everyone knew about our "breakup"
but the pain was stronger in the summer
than with the gossip wildfire.
You weren't worth my energy

and neither was she.
But I made you worth my energy,
channelled through determination
blinded by competition.

Who was I?

I didn't know who I was anymore.

I was no longer the sweet girl
who would've taken a minute to help
someone struggling with their work.

I was no longer the patient girl
who would've explained
material to her classmates.

I was no longer the generous girl
who lavished her classmates
with support in hard times.

I didn't know who I was anymore.

"I wouldn't have told anyone, promise."

I left Economics once, cornered by you
before I could run down the stairs.

You asked me if I was seeing him,
a pointed look to the only guy who had the guts
to challenge you for a hallucinatory love.

Murmured whispers didn't suffice,
us hiding in the garden and I spilled
the truthful tea to make you smile.

Why did I try?
Why was your smile contagious?

"I didn't want to lose you to him, it'd end me."

I didn't want to feel anything from your words
but my heart
slightly fluttered,
gravelling my blood.

I hated the effect you had on me,
especially when you said, "Promise not to tell?"
and I replied, "I wouldn't have told anyone, promise."

"I still love you,"

you were gone.

I knew I was dumb, stop rubbing it in

I knew I should've built my walls
stronger, sturdier, shatterproof.
I knew they'd break the instant
you said something sweet.

I knew I was dumb,
in more ways than one,
but I needed you to stop
rubbing it in.

The bottle broke

Waterworks broke durable dams
when exhausted rocks hid the shore.

The trail was dangerous but so were you.

What would I have chosen?

It wasn't easy pretending,
pretending wasn't easy.

You finally left me alone
and I felt freely trapped.

Your lover strangled my breath
without you but the nozzle
was already tightened.

Confidence + tears = zero

The year closed like the beginning.
But I was emotionless,
fatigued,
enervated.

I didn't care if you or she wanted to destroy me;
my heartbroken sleep paralysis did enough.

I was losing myself,
losing my control,
losing my life.

Grades slipped, friendships ended, and I was a lost cause.

I didn't speak to anyone about what killed me since guilt
ate me inside out daily after years of our past burnt my
neck.
The scarlet letters of your initials reminded me of how
I once belonged to you and the way those times felt.

I was in a cycle where escape was a dream.
I wanted the nightmarish track to end midway.

I knew you had no faith in me

My last assessment became the hot rumour,
spiralling faster than our supposed "breakup".

Was I surprised?

No, I knew.

Your lover was always around,
following and listening to my every word.
I didn't want anyone to know but the
social media wildfire was uncontrollable.

You encouraged lies to spread
when the truth was unknown to you.

Maybe I didn't study enough,
maybe I played it too cool?

But maybe I lost faith in myself too...

Grade 12

Did you accept the real me or the fake me?

You were a ricochet that flew past me
without a second thought to question.
I guessed it wasn't important to know the truth
since you didn't have to keep running non-stop.
You liked the chase, the heat, the game.
You didn't want to accept anything.
You lived by existing blindly,
but your tunnel vision inflicted the greatest agony.
That moment of care took flight at the fired pistol.

You didn't wait, not because love had died out,
but because you didn't know who was
the real me or the fake me.

You should've told the truth

If you felt nothing anymore,
it would've been okay from the start.

But you liked keeping your ploy
of a loveless spell.

You never saw me for who I was
though I wished you could've.
I was an easy match,
a measly opponent
you wished to beat
in your final lap.

I granted your wishes when other genies
failed but I wasn't enough for you.
You should've asked for a final truthful wish
but performed lies better than sprints.

My heart was heavy

Disappointed in you
more than myself,
it wasn't a surprise
since the truth was clear
from the starting line.

My lungs imploded

A volcano awakened.
The trail shook violently
before my mind shut down.
You stirred the magma, the pressure
pushing up the conduit.
The crater made way for the royal
lava, scorching the end ahead.

This was worse each day

I felt my tears
stabbing me this morning,
I felt my muscles
draining life this afternoon,
I felt my heart
stop beating this evening.

Split times were insane,
cadences were inhumane
and you hit the wall.

But I had friends who were staying
and the end in sight was *mine*,

not *yours*.

One more moment, one more lie

You spoke to me after months and I wish you didn't.
I was rebuilding my friendships,
focusing on my grades and having fun again.

But like always, you fractured it all.

"We weren't working out and I missed you."
One more moment, one more lie.

I begged for another lie, lie and say you loved me.

You didn't and my answer was above crystal clear.
I didn't respond, pushing past like nothing occurred.

You called after me, but I didn't hear you,
not this time, not ever again —
both of you silenced.

"I've wanted you back
the moment I lost you,
I made a mistake."

That made two of us.

The dams have broken

It didn't matter anymore
when tears flooded papers,
notes, exams and days.

The dams have broken.

It wasn't your fault only, never.
It was everything pushing the barricades.

You didn't want her but you also
didn't want me too, even if you
said otherwise to my face.

You were Pinocchio but I
didn't plan on stopping your
hanging.

Therapy — what was that?

I was honest when talking about experiences
but therapy from you wasn't another effortless sprint.
An endless relay, pounding my joints.

Therapy from you was a fever dream.

Sometimes I forgot the meaning of therapy
when you clouded my mind from everything.
I was over it now, but past-me struggled hard.

My mindset was critical.

If you asked what therapy was to me,
I'd answer with a mix of music, words, love,
breakdowns, trust, wisdom and acceptance.

Because therapy wasn't one thing for me.

It was finding a dream,
awakening knowing it was mine
without you to play the puppeteer.

You never respected me, so I moved on

There you were, confident like the world didn't crash.

Well, your world never crashed under your control.

You tried talking some '*sense*' into me, but I didn't listen.

There was nothing left for us to say,
not when those words were frivolous
and closure was your 'aching broken heart'.

You never respected me, so why start pretending when
I was happy, free and forgetting you existed?

Your friends moved on
and I did too.

Why *couldn't* you?

There was nothing for us here, time to go.
My energy wasn't wasted on you anymore.

This was my world; this was my life

Comfortable in
my skin since I stopped
waiting for you.

I was in my world
with my life
and my happiness.

I loved myself.

You can't put me down anymore

I was finally myself again.

Wind in hair, feet on gravel,
all those years became
a distant, foggy memory.

I realised you weren't
worth my precious seconds.
I was in control of my life.

You couldn't beat my best
if you tried.

Say what you want, it was your funeral

I went through the five stages of grief after losing you
but those months only left me with greater knowledge,
strength and understanding of who I was and who I am.

Whatever you had left to say was fickle;
it wouldn't settle in stone when your voice echoed.

I was in control, you were abusing my space.
I was thriving strong, you were surviving time.
I was myself, you were another sad guy.

Can you hear me?

I wasn't afraid to stand up for myself.

You silenced me for six years too long,
smothering my potential to blossom;
my independence stalled.

I wasn't scared to put myself out there.

You couldn't have stopped me from writing,
creating art I wanted that may have damaged
your image

but never mine, one you invented.

I was free from your reign.

Can you hear me?

You didn't have a say in my friends or who I
talked to anymore — it was my choice.

And my choice started with a permanent goodbye to you.

I was me and I was proud

I grew into myself on my own accord.
I became the person I needed to be.
I was me and I was proud of who I was.

You were never the one who ran my life.
You didn't live the decisions you made for my life.
You weren't persisting with the events in my life.

I was me *now*.
I was the *real* me.
I was in *love* with the real me.

I found my voice

I was here to stay.
I was here to run proud.
I was here for me.
I was all I needed.

I found my voice.

And no one silenced me.

Thank you for reading *everything i couldn't say*! If you enjoyed the book, I would be beyond grateful if you left a review on any platform of your choice.

Reviews are so beneficial for authors and each one helps!

Love always,
Isabella

Instagram:
@isabellajuanitalyn

TikTok:
@isabellajuanitalyn

YouTube:
www.youtube.com/@isabellajuanitalyn

Acknowledgements

Thank you for reading this poetry collection! I loved composing and creating this beautiful story over the past months, surrounded by the sweetest comments and people ever. Now finally out in the world, I hope you love it as much as I do!

I would love to thank my lovely beta readers Talia, Sonja, and Quindira for the continuous constructive criticism and general improvements to the storyline. Your feedback elevated the poems, and I am thankful for such genuine honesty and focus.

Thank you to my proof editors Rhianna, Olivia, Daniella, and Emma for the immediate responses and attention to detail in tight deadlines. You're the best!

Thank you to Krystal for the wonderful illustrations and cover design. I cannot wait to work with you on future projects and see where our careers go.

And finally, thank you to you, the reader, for showing this book so much love and adoration. I am continuously overjoyed by the constant happiness I receive. You deserve the world!

Love Always,
Isabella

Isabella Juanita Lyn is an author, poet, and digital creator. With a focus on love and heartbreak, her books contain heart-wrenching emotions to help others find themselves. She strives to aspire others to follow their dreams and most importantly, stand up for themselves and their beliefs. Besides writing, reading, and creating content, Isabella is obsessed with piglets and bunnies, learning random things in the world of Economics and Mathematics, and finding joy in life's little things.